COURT OF REBELS

Laura Shenton

COURT OF REBELS

Laura Shenton

Iridescent Toad Publishing

Iridescent Toad Publishing.

Cover by Real Life Design.

First edition. ISBN: 978-1-913779-84-9

Chapter One

"Catch you later then," he said.

It was the same as always, and, just as he always did, Tyal walked jauntily over to the bar. He would be spending the evening there, expecting me to keep out of the way. He could have just as easily opted to frequent the tavern alone, but that wasn't his way. He often expected me to go with him. That way, he could keep an eye on me.

The tavern was noisy, humid and sweaty – even on what was a relatively cool summer's evening. Tyal had instructed me to go and dance. On the packed floor, I could barely manage to move amongst the other fae women without having to hunch my shoulders and retract my wings.

Although the dance floor was only at the other side of the room, I was pleased to be away from Tyal for a bit. I had been matched with him just two years ago and already I'd had enough. It always made me cringe to think that one day I would have to marry him. Sadly, for most of the fae women in Blackfern, that was simply the way things had always been.

I had been matched with Tyal on account of factors that were out of my hands, for the law in Blackfern was one that had stood for generations. On the day of their twenty-first birthday, all female fae were to be assigned a male suitor – whether they liked them, or indeed, couldn't stand them.

There was nothing particularly likeable about Tyal. He wasn't an attractive man; his nose was crooked, his eyes bulged out in comparison to the rest of his thinly-sculpted features. Even when he smiled, he looked like he was smirking vindictively. In the grand scheme of things, they were all aspects that I would have been able to overlook. They were all things that could easily go unnoticed after a while. A person's bad attitude though, had always been something that I had never been able to overlook, and once I had been exposed to Tyal's, my disgust for the man had grown to be constant.

Tyal was typical of the entitled male fae of Blackfern. He was the type who would turn up late to a banquet, address the most anxious-looking server there, and demand to have a particular delicacy prepared especially. Such was the extent of Tyal's sense of entitlement, that either he didn't care about upsetting people, or perhaps there was even a part of him that enjoyed having that kind of power.

Tyal had always felt that he had a special right to get his own way, even if it was at the expense and misfortune of somebody else – somebody lower in the rankings of the way the kingdom's society was structured.

Although not entirely through my own choice, I continued to dance to the band that was playing. It was a relief to be away from Tyal as more of his drinking buddies gathered around him. I didn't feel that I was missing anything. I suspected that he valued what they had to say over and above what I did. He had never listened to me, but in a way, I was ok with that. Truthfully, in knowing that he would never have the propensity to be able to understand me anyway, I had nothing to say to him.

It wasn't unusual for fae women to gather on the dance floor while the men carried on downing their goblets of mead. Although between us, we had little in common, there was a sense of solidarity. With the exception of my cousin, Lyda, I had never been close to any of the other women in Blackfern, and I was ok with that.

I had always lived in Blackfern, and not through my own choice; that's where I was born. With the exception of the few who managed to escape, to be born in Blackfern, was to die in Blackfern. Very few fae ever left Blackfern. Those who worked for the king would occasionally venture out with special permission – sometimes on an errand to explore other places and to keep an eye on an enemy court, or sometimes to get supplies from other nearby, authorised traders. Rarely did anybody get to frequent the land that surrounded the perimeter of Blackfern. It was simply unheard of. To attempt to do it without permission was to put your life at risk. Anybody not sentenced to death by public execution, would be locked up in the most horrible of prisons. There were several throughout Blackfern. Some of them were labour camps, whilst others were simply cells in which captives would perish.

Some of the fae in Blackfern had always been reluctant to believe the horrors of what happened in the kingdom's prisons. Many fae were, in fact, proud to call Blackfern their home. Either they were privileged, or they were lucky enough to be naive as to what was happening. Many of them were compliant and not willing to question anything. Even then though, with Blackfern being the dictatorship that it was, it wasn't unusual for the perfectly innocent to end up in some kind of trouble. For me, to even voice the fact that I didn't want to be with Tyal would be an insult to the king's way of doing things, and would probably see me taken away in the middle of the night by several fae stronger than me.

The laws of Blackfern were rigid and the kingdom's enforcement of them was strict. There was nothing that I, or anyone else I knew, could do about it. It was simply the case that by fortune of birth, some fae thrived, some barely survived, and others… well, it wasn't good.

The tavern band played the melodies of their folk songs beautifully. I had always loved music. The fae of Blackfern were allowed to enjoy it, just so long as it wasn't composed or played against the terms set by the kingdom. In taverns in particular, folk bands were encouraged to play; an entertained and inebriated society was a placated one. Creativity certainly hadn't been banned in Blackfern, and I was grateful for that. It was always a joy to get lost in music because it gave my mind a chance to wander, if only for a brief interlude of time. All the same though, it was impossible to feel truly free.

I looked over at the bar. Tyal was still surrounded by his drinking buddies. Compared to some of them, he actually looked incredibly focused – more so than was usual for a typical Friday night. Just as he looked up at me from his goblet, I diverted my eyes away. I didn't want to be accused of trying to get involved with matters that didn't concern me. Tyal had always made it very clear that whilst I was there to accompany him, I wasn't there to engage with anything that he deemed to be his business only. As he continued to talk with his acquaintances, I kept my head down, turning my focus back to the music as an older male fae played a beautiful song on his tin whistle.

As a younger-looking fae finished the song with her fiddle, everyone on the dance floor gave the band a round of applause, appreciating their work and the music. When I looked around the room once more, Tyal whistled loudly at me in that condescending way that he always did, beckoning me to come and sit by him. It made me squirm to think that this wouldn't come to any good; it was only ever uncomfortable when I got summoned to sit with him and his cohorts. None of them had much tact, but then they had never needed to have any, what with being relatively privileged and having had women handed to them by birthright.

Once at the bar, I started to glance around for a stool to perch myself on, but thought better of it. I didn't want to get too comfortable and end up having to sit there all night.

Tyal bent forward towards me, making it very clear that he didn't want anyone else to hear what he was saying.

"Listen, Skyler," he said, his face so close to mine that I could smell the foul odour of his breath. "I'm going outside for a bit to talk with Phoenix. Don't follow me. Just wait for me to come back. Ok?"

It wasn't a question. It was an instruction.

"Yeah, sure. No worries," I said unconvincingly. "Not a problem."

Of course, it *was* a problem; this wasn't typical of Tyal's normal behaviour. Usually by this point in the night, he would have been too drunk to string a coherent sentence together. On this occasion though, he seemed abnormally vigilant. I decided that my best bet was to simply comply in the hope that everything would be ok.

***

Tyal came back to the bar looking abrasive and determined. He motioned to me that it was time to leave. As he ushered me out of the tavern with him, I was happy to get out into the fresh air, even if it did mean that he and I would be alone once more as we headed off on the journey home.

Just as I had been hoping for, the cool breeze of the forest at night felt soothing against my skin. As I looked up to see a flock of birds flying up high over the trees, I noticed the apples that hung from the branches. As I imagined how crisp and fresh they would be upon the first bite, it made me crave them. I wanted to ask Tyal if he would be ok with me removing one from a branch, but with his state of focus being so rigid, it didn't seem like the best thing to do.

"Listen," he instructed me, just as he often did, his voice low. "We need to have a talk when we get home."

He looked over his shoulder, clearly anxious of the possibility that he could be overheard. I simply nodded. I didn't want to say or do anything to provoke his temper; it wasn't worth it. Besides, no matter what it was that needed to be said, *nothing* was worth the risk of being overheard.

16

Chapter Two

It was just the two of us back home. I was grateful for the fact that I hadn't been expected to birth a child for Tyal yet. Even though it had been determined by the regime that I must be with him, I had always had this great hope in the back of my mind that something – *anything* – would grant me the freedom of being able to get away from him. Our humble home, which had been provided by the dictatorship of Blackfern, was sufficient enough. It was much better than what many of the fae had come to accept as the norm. Although I appreciated the comforts of having a nice bed, a kitchen, and a cellar stocked with various meats, cheeses and jams, none of that was enough to compensate for the thought of what a future with Tyal would look like.

As I buttered bread from the fresh loaf that we were about to eat, I took the opportunity to look out of the window. Apart from a few fireflies, there was little movement to be seen outside. All of the forest animals had settled down for the night. I told myself that regardless of what it was that Tyal needed to tell me, I would simply have to go along with it.

"We're going to cross the border in the early hours of Sunday morning," he said frankly, trying to sound calm.

"What?!" I exclaimed, struggling to contain my emotion. "That's… That's crazy! Why? Why would we do that?"

"It's ok," he said insistently, unfazed by my fear. "I've been given an opportunity to bring in some goods to trade on the black market."

"But why would you do that?!" I asked, still horrified. "Everything you need is given to you by the king. Why would you betray that? Why take such a risk, just for a pittance of gold that we would have to hide? I mean, really, what are a few more coins compared to the risk of being caught and having to face goodness knows what consequences?"

Tyal laughed indignantly.

"We'll be fine," he said. "This is going to be worth it. I've worked hard all my life, and I really think I deserve a little bit more. We'll be able to afford nicer things. You'd like that, wouldn't you?"

My mind was whirling. I couldn't stop Tyal from making a stupid decision. Simply by factor of association though, if he were to get caught, it would also put my life in danger.

"Besides," he added. "You'll know what to do. If anything looks like it's about to go wrong, you can create a distraction."

I had no words for this. Tyal's sense of entitlement had always been insulting and the fact that he was hankering for more spoke volumes about the kind of person he was. I didn't want to get involved, but I had no choice. It made my stomach turn. Not only did I feel sick, but I was infuriated. I just couldn't get my head around what he was asking me to do, and yet deep down, I knew that he wasn't messing about.

"On Sunday morning, we're going to get moving just before sunrise," he explained. "Once I've crossed the border into Ovon, it should only take me twenty minutes or so, and then I'll be back in Blackfern. All I'm going to do is get some exotic fruit and some cashmere to bring back and trade. Phoenix has reliably informed me that the guards on duty at the border during that time are not the most vigilant. They are the weaker of the king's army, bullied into taking the shift that the more experienced guards don't want. It's the perfect opportunity for us."

I cringed at Tyal's confidence, and indeed, at his delusional mentality. Attempting to cross the border just to get into Ovon was risky enough. Any fae who could get away with that alone would be pushing their luck. But to expect to get back into Blackfern without capture and arrest? It was unfathomable!

Why would any fae be so crazy as to come back to Blackfern after having set foot in the safety of Ovon? If someone is going to take the risk of breaching the threshold into Ovon, then surely they would only do so with the intention of staying there – not to come back to Blackfern with a few meagre items to trade!

But then it dawned on me: Tyal was happy with his life in Blackfern. Whilst he was very much on his own team, he also knew where his bread was buttered – and not the kind that I was preparing for us to eat!

As he continued to ramble on about why he was so sure of his plan, I started to daydream about how wonderful it would be to get out of Blackfern forever.

Tyal finished whatever it was that he'd wanted to say to me, and then told me that it was time for bed. I settled down under the woven quilt that I had crafted out of supplies from the forest. When he got in bed next to me, I had already closed my eyes, pretending to be asleep. I hoped that he wouldn't want anything from me. He repulsed me in every way.

As the effects of whatever alcohol he had consumed took its toll on him, Tyal was soon fast asleep. Grateful for the time it granted me to be alone with my thoughts, I began to rationalise the situation I was in.

I had always been smarter than Tyal. I had always done well at school, but no fae woman in Blackfern had ever been allowed to put their intelligence to any real use. Despite how stupid I thought his plan was, if he wanted me to go to the border with him, then I would have no say in it.

I'm going to have to be smart about this. If Tyal is so damn certain about his plan, and if I really do find myself at the border and it starts to go dangerously wrong, I'm going to have to think fast.

Chapter Three

Since being matched with Tyal, Saturdays had always been a good day for me. He would typically spend them drinking at the tavern or going out alone to hunt. Either way, I liked them because they granted me some time to myself.

Considering what Tyal was planning, I was surprised that he hadn't locked me inside the cottage, firmly instructing me not to leave. Perhaps he had been so focused on other things that keeping an eye on me hadn't been his main priority. It suited me just fine because on this particular Saturday, I needed to go and see Lyda, if only to get a sense of normalcy.

It was always a pleasure to go and have tea with Lyda. In terms of who she had been matched with for a husband, she had been lucky. Dundryl was incredibly easy-going, intelligent and patient. The dictatorship had placed him in a comfortable clerical role. He didn't have the same brutality about him that some of the men who worked for the kingdom did. As a result, Lyda's life was relatively pleasant and relaxed.

"I've had a nice week," Lyda said as she nursed her cup of tea, gesturing at the beautiful flora and fauna surrounding us. "The weather has been perfect for using watercolours outside and the garden has been a brilliant source of inspiration."

She continued to elaborate on the joys of her hobbies, which Dundryl's income had been able to comfortably facilitate. Soon though, she sat forward on her log and looked at me with one eyebrow raised.

"You don't seem like yourself today, Skyler. I can't quite put my finger on it, but you seem distant somehow."

It wasn't safe to tell her what was on my mind whilst we were still outside, but going inside to talk wasn't an option either. I couldn't run the risk of Dundryl overhearing anything. However, Lyda and I had always been close. If anything terrible were to happen to me, I couldn't bear the thought of her not knowing.

"Listen," I said, keeping my voice as quiet as I possibly could. "I need to tell you something. And I'm begging you, please, please, *please* don't tell anybody. What I'm about to say could implicate you, but the thought of not telling you scares me all the same."

Lyda had always been able to read me like a book. She knew I was struggling to stay composed. She put her hand on mine and looked deep into my eyes.

"Take some deep breaths," she said. "Stay calm and think about what it is you need to say."

Lyda and I had always been able to tell each other everything. But this was different. I didn't want her to know about something that could put her in danger. The thought of her being interrogated flashed through my mind and made me shudder. Equally though, I couldn't bear to think that should I be captured and imprisoned, or simply killed on the spot, she would forever be left to question what had happened to me.

"Tyal wants us to go over the border," I blurted out in a desperate whisper.

"What do you mean?!" Lyda asked, managing to keep her voice low despite her shock. "Don't be silly!"

"He wants to go into Ovon to get some goods, and then come straight back," I said. "It's not a trip that he has been authorised to take. He's adamant that he wants to start trading on the black market. He has insisted that I go with him."

"That's awful," said Lyda. "And really, I guess there's nothing you can do to get out of it. I mean, even if you were to stay at home whilst Tyal went to the border, you would still be guilty by association."

I thought about Lyda's comment for a moment. She was right. There was nothing I could do to avoid becoming implicated by Tyal. The whole situation was incredibly dangerous.

Lyda looked around sharply, suspiciously checking that we were not within earshot of anyone else. As happy as she was in her marriage to Dundryl, she knew that if he were to overhear our conversation, it could have grave consequences. Although she had a reasonably good rapport with her husband, she had the intelligence to think for herself; she had always known what to share, and what to keep from him.

"I'm not going to tell anybody about any of this," she said. "I just wish so damn much that something could be done to get you out of this situation. It's awful that you are getting dragged into this against your will."

"I know," I said. "I don't want to go with Tyal. He's a moron and this idea of his is terrifying. Look, I've only told *you* about this because I need to know that if anything bad happens to me, you won't be in the dark about it. I wouldn't want you to think that I was wilfully engaged in this. Or worse still, I wouldn't want you to find out the hard way that something bad had happened to me; I wouldn't want you to hear about it on the grapevine and then be left to imagine all kinds of horror."

"This isn't your fault," Lyda replied, sensing how upset I was. "You didn't ask for this."

"You know what Tyal's like," I said. "Once he gets it in his head that he is going to do something, there's no stopping him. He can't get over this idea of his that he deserves more than what the king gives him."

"He's an idiot," said Lyda, struggling to keep her voice down. "He has been lucky in terms of his rank. He has everything that he could ever need, and yet he is choosing to put you both in danger for just a little bit more. It's disgusting."

Lyda and I looked at each other and nodded twice. It had always been our code signal to stop talking. If anyone outside overheard us, they would be obliged to report us to the regime. In not doing so, they could put themselves in danger. As my mother had always said when we were growing up, even the trees have ears.

"I wish I could help you," Lyda whispered carefully, full of fear and remorse. "I'm so sorry that I can't. This is agonising for me. All I can do is pray to the fae gods that you come out of this ok, or better yet, that Tyal will come to his senses before the morning."

Chapter Four

Just as we had been hoping for, the forest was silent. There was nobody else around. As we walked along the dirt path, the air felt fresh, but there was no breeze. Even the smallest tree branches and their abundance of lush leaves seemed rigidly still.

The sun had yet to rise and the birds had yet to sing. We had packed everything the night before: we mostly had small bags inside our main bags in order to carry the goods back from Ovon.

Tyal had sternly instructed me that all I needed to do was follow his lead. I wasn't to say anything; I was to always look to him for guidance regarding what I should do next.

"Just follow my lead and everything will be ok," he said. "If in doubt, just watch what I do and copy me."

I simply nodded, keen to show him that I didn't want anything to go wrong.

"Skyler, you can't look so nervous," he said. "If you look like that when we get to the border, we will be suspected straight away."

He looked around cautiously, realising that he needed to lower his voice.

"The guards currently on duty are not the most experienced. They're not the brightest either," he continued. "When they question us, just go along with what I say and everything will be fine."

I didn't share his confidence. With every step I took, I was all too aware that I could be walking towards a doomed fate. I expected that at the very least, one or both of us would have to face some kind of interrogation.

It made me angry to think that I was having to go through all of this just because Tyal was so greedy. We had a home and we never went without food.

Why the hell is he so willing to risk our lives for something so meagre?

Perhaps it wasn't even about resources. Perhaps he simply wanted to challenge authority. Even though he complied with the dictatorship and largely benefitted from how it operated, there was a part of him that wanted to push the boundaries of what he could get away with. His ego had never done him any good.

I took a deep breath, desperate to calm my fear, which was rapidly turning into a state of anger.

How dare he put us in this situation?! I didn't ask for any of this!

As we ventured further towards the border, I noticed that the trees were closer together. Nothing for civilisation had been built or developed on this part of the forest. In fact, it looked as though extra trees and bushes may have been planted to block Blackfern's view of the courts beyond it; the regime had probably gone to great lengths to conceal the knee-high ditch that all fae knew about anyway. If not for the brutality of the dictatorship, the low, dry ground would have been easy for anyone to walk across into a neighbouring court.

Although I had no idea what may be beyond the border, I was certain that it couldn't be any worse than the interrogation that we were potentially about to face.

"I'm pretty sure the guards must be in that hut up ahead," Tyal whispered. "I'm going to go up to the hatch and declare my business to them."

I nodded reluctantly, and, soon enough, we found ourselves standing before the hatch of the small hut. It was occupied by two guards, neither of whom appeared to be naive or incompetent. Both male fae, they were each armed with not only a bow and arrow, but ropes, hammers, and blades. Their expressions cynical and their bodies muscular, neither of them looked like the youngest of recruits. I was beginning to wonder whether Tyal – or perhaps his suspicious-looking acquaintance, Phoenix – had made some tremendously inaccurate assumptions about who would be guarding the border on this particular shift.

"State your business, in the name of the king," one of the guards demanded loudly, his voice gruff and intimidating.

The guard was evidently used to the procedure

that he was about to undertake. Tyal steadied himself, keen to come across as calm and collected. He could be very manipulative when he needed to be.

"Good morning, gentlemen," he said. "I'm just passing by on an errand for the king. I've got my paperwork in my bag. Would you like to see it?"

"Certainly," said the other guard, his tone matter-of-fact and giving nothing away.

After faffing around in the large pocket of his bag, Tyal took out a scroll. He unravelled it, and then slapped it down on the ledge of the hatch.

As the guards scanned their eyes across the abundance of scrawled words on the parchment, the tense silence was excruciating. By the time the more vocal of the two finally spoke, I felt as though I was going to pass out in fear.

"Ok," he said, a hand still on the document as he addressed Tyal. "That all seems to be in order. And will your lady be crossing the border with you?"

Another awkward silence. As I glanced at Tyal's

expression, it occurred to me that he might have failed to account for anyone but himself on his dodgy paperwork.

Mustering up the same style of false bravado that had served him for most of his life, Tyal puffed out his chest and spoke with his crooked nose held high.

"I can't see how taking my woman over the border would be a problem, gentlemen. There was no paperwork issued for her, but she will certainly be helpful to the errand that *I* have been authorised to go on. She will be able to carry extra supplies that I have been asked to acquire. You don't need me to tell you that a lack of resources would be costly to Blackfern."

The two guards looked at each other. I was struggling to tell whether they were unconvinced by Tyal's explanation, or simply just annoyed at the arrogance with which he was conducting himself.

"Wait there," said the quieter guard.

With that, they rolled down the heavy shutters of the hatch, clearly wishing to talk amongst themselves.

With the guards unable to see us, Tyal sharply nudged me. He looked at me with a hard glare, almost as if blaming me for the problems with his fraudulent paperwork.

My mind was racing. In that moment, I wished that I could communicate with him – either through a code signal like that which I had with Lyda, or telepathically through my magic. Neither was an option though. The former wasn't possible through a lack of rapport with Tyal, and the latter would get me arrested immediately. Long ago, the fae of Blackfern had been banned from using their magic. Besides, I wasn't even sure if I still had the ability.

My thoughts were interrupted by the abrasive noise of the hatch being opened.

"We're going to check a few things," said the louder guard, addressing Tyal. "We will ask your lady some questions."

The beat of my heart thumped rapidly in my mouth. Everything around me began to spin. I felt sick to my core.

This is it! They're going to interrogate me!

"Very well," said Tyal, sounding almost disturbingly calm about my predicament.

With speed and efficiency, and before I had time to even take a deep breath, the two guards were outside the hut. They took me by the arms and marched me back in with them, leaving Tyal outside.

The inside of the hut was cramped and dark. It was too early in the day to light candles and the sun hadn't fully risen. I had no time to take in my surroundings as the guards made me sit down on an old wooden chair.

"Ok," said the more talkative guard, his tone more relaxed than when he had been addressing Tyal. "It's clear that you're not supposed to be on this errand. Have you got anything to say for yourself?"

It almost seemed that the guard wanted to help me. I didn't feel that he was trying to trick me. It was as though he genuinely wanted to talk.

No! I mustn't say anything! I can't let myself be fooled. Surely this is just their way of lulling me into a false sense of security so that I will tell them anything and everything.

The fear and confusion of the situation was so overwhelming that I found myself unable to speak. I started to shake and cry. I didn't want them to look at me, but I was too scared to cover my face with my hands. I needed to stay alert. I had no idea what they were about to do to me.

Can't breathe! Can't breathe! Oh God! I'm having a panic attack!

"I don't know anything! I don't know anything! I'm so sorry," I blurted out. "I don't. I just don't know."

Slowly and carefully, the guard crouched down and put a hand on my knee. He looked up at me and spoke softly.

"Skyler."

He knows my name?!

"You don't know us," he continued. "But we're here to help you. With Tyal outside and unable to hear us, we can drop the act now. We're on your side. You need to know that you're here because Phoenix has set Tyal up. There is no black market deal opportunity. Phoenix simply used Tyal in order to get you here. We came up with a story that the goods to be bought over the border were simply too great and too many for just one pair of hands to carry."

"What?!" I exclaimed. "Is Tyal going to be ok?!"

Although I didn't have any true feelings for Tyal, I couldn't bear the thought of something terrible happening to him.

"Tyal is going to be fine," soothed the other guard. "We will simply tell him to go home. As far as we're concerned, there is nothing to report."

"The priority now, is you," said the guard in front of me. "We have worked hard to make this happen and an opportunity like this is a one-off. The coast is clear for you to go over the border. We want to help you escape into Ovon."

"But why?" I asked, alarmed at the scale of the decision I was being invited to make. "My family are all here in Blackfern. I can't say that I have never thought of it, but who am I to go over the border?"

"The real question is, why would you want to

stay here in Blackfern? Your parents passed away long ago. Lyda will be fine because Dundryl is a good provider and a decent enough man."

"How do you know about Lyda?" I asked, annoyed that someone may have been spying.

"Look, we can't keep talking," the guard in front of me said hastily. "Do you want to go over the border, or don't you?"

"I don't even know what's over there," I replied. "All I've heard are stories and rumours. And anyway, how can I trust you? How can I be sure that you're not just trying to set me up so that it looks like you're doing your job? We all know that some of the king's guards will do anything in a desperate attempt to give themselves an advantage."

"You're right," he replied. "You can't truly trust anyone; you can't trust us, and you can't even trust him who's waiting for you out there. The best you can do is listen to your instincts. Take a leap of faith, and hope for the best."

"But what if I were to cross the border and then find myself wanting to come back?" I asked.

It was a reasonable question. Anybody trying to get back into Blackfern after having left would immediately face punishment for having betrayed the regime in the first place.

"I think you're just going to have to put your confidence in us," said the guard in front of me as he stood up.

Immediately, the glow of magic began to radiate from both guards, their hands illuminated by a light that was almost blinding. Together, they softly pressed down on my shoulders. I started to panic again, realising that I couldn't move. A wave of exhaustion cascaded over me, and then, everything quickly faded into nothingness.

Chapter Five

As I opened my eyes, all I could see was leaves and branches before a bright blue sky. I quickly realised that I was flat on my back.

Where am I?

I could barely move. I started to panic.

"Help!" I shouted.

Still disorientated, within my blurry field of vision, I could suddenly see the silhouette of a fae I had never seen before.

"I think you're still confused," I heard her say. "It's ok. You will soon come around. I just need to give you a bit of time."

"Who? W-what?" I stammered, still afraid and

not knowing if I could trust the unfamiliar fae beside me.

"What matters now, is that despite how the odds were so against us, we have managed to get you here," she said.

"What? Where am I?"

The female fae, probably around the same age as myself, crouched down and got closer to me. Her long brown hair was tied back, revealing a pretty face. She smiled at me reassuringly and rummaged around in her bag, eventually pulling out an apple.

"Here," she said. "Eat this. You look like you need it."

As I sat up and started to get my bearings of the forest around me, I remembered that I had skipped breakfast. Tyal had been so keen for us to leave the cottage that it simply hadn't crossed my mind at the time.

I nodded and accepted the apple. Gratefully, I took a bite. It was crisp and refreshing.

"I thought you'd need that," she said. "I always

make sure to bring some food with me when bringing someone over the border from Blackfern. The sheer emotion of it can be exhausting for some."

"So I'm not in Blackfern anymore?" I asked. "But that must mean…"

"Yes," she cut in. "You're in Ovon now. I'm Aybel, by the way."

She extended her arm out to me and took my hand in hers, pulling me up to a standing position.

"It's ok," she said. "Take your time, and when you're ready to move, we'll head to the cottage."

Although I felt reasonably safe in Aybel's company, a part of me was upset that I had been transported across the border. The idea wasn't one that I had ever been *entirely* against, but ultimately, the decision had been taken out of my hands when the guards had used their magic on me. I hadn't asked for this.

What if I want to go back to Blackfern? What about Lyda?

Chapter Six

The little cottage that I found myself in was one of the most beautiful that I'd ever seen – even more so than Dundryl's.

"Wow!" I said. "You must be really high-up in the order here."

Aybel laughed awkwardly.

"Not really," she said. "Everything that we have is truly our own. It's not based on what any kind of regime or dictatorship decides for us. Here in Ovon, we can do what we want. As long as we're not hurting anybody else, our lifestyle is very much up to us."

"That's amazing," I said.

"We have artists and doctors and everything in between here, just like you do in Blackfern," she continued. "The difference here though, is that unlike the fae of Blackfern, everyone here in Ovon makes their own choices; we don't have to fulfil any particular role in life simply because a regime has bullied us into it."

It was a lot to take in. I had heard about what the courts outside of Blackfern might be like, but never in my wildest dreams had I truly been able to visualise what they might feel like in reality. Aybel seemed at ease with her lot in life. Not only that, but she had a reassuring energy about her. I had already sensed that she was trustworthy. Although I was still feeling confused and didn't truly understand why I had been brought to Ovon, as I watched Aybel heat some water on the stove to make us some elderberry tea, I was satisfied that I wasn't in the worst of places by any means.

"I think you must have met Phoenix already," Aybel said as she tinkered around in the cupboards.

"Kind of," I replied. "I haven't really spoken to him before though."

"He has been instrumental in getting you over the border."

"I can't understand why he would take such a risk. I always had him down as being loyal to Blackfern."

"You would think so," Aybel said, clearly in the know. "He does a great job of convincing the fae of Blackfern that he is loyal to the regime there. And rightly so! He would be in grave danger if any of the Blackfern loyalists were to find out otherwise."

"Why would anyone want to put themselves in such a position?" I asked.

I was almost angry that someone would put their life on the line like that, and all the more so in how they had decided to get me involved.

"Why would he go to all that trouble?" I asked. "Besides, what does he care about me? He barely even knows me."

"We just want to help," said Aybel, carefully putting a cup of sweetly-scented tea on the table in front of me.

I had my doubts, but I didn't wish to offend my host. She hadn't given me any cause to distrust her. As I sipped my tea, the soothing brew awakened my senses and warmed me to the core.

Suddenly, there was a rhythmic tapping against the window of the cottage.

"Ah," said Aybel. "That will be him now."

"Who?" I asked. "Phoenix?"

"Yes," she replied as she happily pranced on her way to open the door.

"Skyler!" Phoenix exclaimed as he walked inside, extending his arms and wings in greeting. "Fantastic! I'm so glad you're here!"

"I don't understand," I said, flatly and a little offended at the slight arrogance in his demeanour.

He pulled out a chair and sat down at the table, shuffling closer towards me. He had a charisma about him that was impossible to ignore.

"Listen," he said. "Do you remember when I spoke to Tyal at the tavern that night?"

"Yes," I said. "I can't forget that. I've been

worried and on edge ever since."

I started to look around nervously before I remembered that I was no longer in Blackfern. In Ovon, no fae lived in fear of saying the wrong thing and being overheard.

"Let me explain," Phoenix said. "The plan was never to get Tyal over the border. All of this has been done to help you."

I didn't know what to make of what I was being told. Although I had never really felt that Tyal was on my side, I certainly didn't like the thought of him being left behind in Blackfern – especially should he end up having to face the consequences of his insubordination to the regime.

"I just can't understand why you would choose to put so many people in so much danger," I said. "Why are you both so invested in this? Neither of you really know me. Why take the risk? And why *me*?"

Having finished washing some dishes, Aybel came over and put her hand on Phoenix's shoulder.

"I have always been an activist," she said. "I guess it's just in my nature. Phoenix did most of the planning to get you out of Blackfern though. We have worked together on this, but he took the biggest risk what with how he has crossed the border quite a few times now."

"That's crazy!" I exclaimed.

"I don't think it is," Phoenix replied patiently. "The time I spend in Ovon, or indeed, any other court that surrounds Blackfern, is time when I am in no danger at all. Nowhere but Blackfern is a dictatorship. Whenever I am there, I always stay vigilant – not only for my own safety, but in order to spot potential allies. I have been watching you for a while now, Skyler. Every time I've seen you, I've been able to read you like a book. Whenever Tyal takes you along to the tavern with him, you look tired and miserable. More than that though, it is clear to me that you have the intelligence to *question* the world around you. I sense that you are perhaps annoyed with me for having brought you here into Ovon, but deep down, you *know* you can't thrive in Blackfern."

"Why me?" I demanded. "Of all the fae you could have brought into Ovon, *why me*?"

"I have always sensed there is something about you that yearns for something better," he replied. "The sad reality for many of the Blackfern fae is that although deep down, they aren't at ease with the regime, they don't have the drive to question it. I couldn't bear the thought of you being stuck there for the rest of your life. I have been wanting to liberate a few fae from Blackfern for a while now. I knew I could reach for you based on your connection to Tyal – simple, gullible, entitled Tyal – who I knew would be easy to manipulate."

Rarely did I find myself lost for words, but Phoenix's explanation had left me speechless, a flood of emotions rushing through my mind. There was no denying that I was flattered that someone had seen potential in me, but equally, I was so damn angry; I felt used.

How dare someone take me away from all that I've ever known? Is this more about their agenda than what's best for me?

I took a deep breath. I had never truly experienced free will before and in many ways, being in Ovon felt no different.

"I can't understand why you would put

yourselves in danger."

"I have enough of a rapport with the King of Blackfern that he's completely blind to what I'm doing," said Phoenix. "I can charm him effectively enough so as not to raise suspicion. He knows nothing about my life in Ovon. He firmly believes that I am passionately dedicated to his god-awful regime."

"Aren't you afraid of being found out?"

"I admit that I'm not fearless. That would be unnatural. I know what the consequences of being caught would be. Whether imprisoned or sentenced to death, I would be tortured mercilessly either way. Of course I am afraid," Phoenix clarified, his voice full of emotion. "More than that though, I am driven by an absolute need to take action. I am in a position to help. If I can save even just a few fae from Blackfern's regime, I think the risk is worth it. I simply can't sit back and pretend everything is ok when clearly it isn't."

"I agree," said Aybel. "Nobody knows what the meaning of this life is. All we can do is try our best to be good – whatever that looks like for us and our beliefs. I'm not saying it's easy, but surely anything worthwhile was never meant to be easy."

"Ok," I said. "I hear what you're saying. I still don't know how I feel about it all. This is a lot for me to take in."

"I promise that we do appreciate your feelings," she said. "Although it's not something that I have ever been through myself, I recognise that this must be difficult for you."

Sweet Aybel's heart was in the right place. Although I felt overwhelmed by the situation, her acknowledgement reminded me of how both she and Phoenix were caring and considerate fae.

I started to think of everything I had left behind in Blackfern. As thoughts of Lyda entered my mind, I broke down and started to cry.

"Lyda could be in trouble," I blurted out between panicked gulps.

"Lyda is going to be fine," said Phoenix. "You didn't tell her about what Tyal was planning, did you?"

My hesitation must have made it obvious that prior to turning up at the border, I had told Lyda *everything*.

"Ok," Phoenix said decisively. "Do you think Lyda has told anybody else?"

I thought carefully for a moment. Lyda had a good relationship with Dundryl, but I also knew that she wouldn't be so foolish as to tell him everything – especially with regards to me. She had been aware for a good while that I wasn't happy with Tyal and that I needed to be able to talk to her in confidence.

"I trust Lyda with my secrets," I said, sniffling and just about managing to compose myself. "I can't imagine that she would have repeated our conversation to anyone else."

Aybel anxiously chewed on her lower lip. She didn't seem convinced. Perhaps her awareness of the betrayals and injustices in Blackfern had made her cynical.

"Ok," Phoenix said assertively. "We'll have to take your word for it. Would you like to bring Lyda over the border?"

"Wow!" I said. "This is a lot to take in."

The question was unexpected. I simply had no idea how to answer it.

"You need to get some rest," Aybel said softly. "You look exhausted. There's a bed for you upstairs. Make yourself at home. If there's anything you need – food, drinks, extra blankets – I'm confident that we'll be able to give you more than you ever had in Blackfern."

I didn't appreciate the insinuation that I had never had anything good in my life. Whilst Aybel's hospitality was coming from a place of kindness, I felt a little insulted about some of the assumptions that she seemed to be making. My life in Blackfern hadn't been entirely horrible. My parents had always cared for me as well as they could have done. Even with Tyal, I had never gone without any of the material things I needed.

All things considered, I couldn't afford to be too proud. As the room started spinning and the slow rhythm of exhaustion began to pound away at my head, I knew it would be foolish to refuse the offer of a bed, and indeed, a comfortable place to stay.

Chapter Seven

As we walked through the forest, the warmth of the afternoon sun felt soothing on my bare shoulders. There was a lovely breeze in the air. It carried upon it the faint sound of music from afar.

"You should come with us," Aybel had said. "If you're going to be staying here for a while, then you may as well become acquainted with Ovon."

I hadn't given any thought to the future. Having only recently stirred from a deep slumber, I wasn't sure if just a few hours – or a whole day and night – had passed. I had opened my eyes to see Aybel sitting patiently on the end of the bed, a small bowl of broth in her hands. When she had passed it to me, she had keenly mentioned that it would be good for me to go out with them, further into the forests of Ovon.

I didn't really feel like being around other fae, but I figured it would be better than staying in the cottage on my own. With everything that had happened, I didn't want to sit indoors worrying, spiralling down a never-ending staircase of irrational thoughts and fears. A life under the regime of Blackfern had taught me that it was vital to keep calm and rational, even in the face of some of the most unexpected situations.

As Aybel, Phoenix and I moved further into the depths of the forest ahead of us, the music grew louder. An abundance of exotic melodies echoed all around. The sound of mass conversation was just as vibrant as the music itself, suggesting that the crowd was large and joyous.

"Cheer up, Skyler," said Phoenix, having sensed my reluctance. "This will be fun. I'm sure you'll enjoy it."

Struggling to be convincing in my response, I smiled at him. I wanted to play along. There was nothing to be gained in being objectionable.

We pushed through some bushes, and upon stepping into the centre of a thick gathering of trees, I was shocked to see just how many fae were present. What also surprised me was how happy they all seemed. Men and women were dancing together, and nobody looked as though they were there under obligation or duress. Everyone seemed so at ease with each other.

Is this all for show? Are they all just putting on a front?

I abruptly shook my head, willing myself to snap out of my paranoid thoughts and keen to remember that not everywhere was like Blackfern.

What I was witnessing was strange and unfamiliar. In a way, it made me feel like more of an outsider than I had before. I needed to remind myself that the festivities going on around me were simply part of day-to-day life for the fae of Ovon. They hadn't grown up in an oppressive environment.

As I began to wonder whether any of the other fae around me had escaped from Blackfern, my thoughts were soon interrupted when Aybel grabbed my hand and walked me over to a buffet table.

"Here," she said as she thrust a goblet of mead into my hand. "Drink up."

When she noticed that I was looking at it quizzically, she smiled softly.

"There's no alcohol in this," she said. "Everyone here is happy, simply because they are. They're not inebriated."

I wouldn't have minded if they were, of course; that wouldn't have been a problem at all. I had simply never been among such a large gathering of fae where everybody seemed genuinely happy to be there. It was nothing like the tavern back in Blackfern, where an air of doubt, uncertainty and paranoia always overshadowed even the relatively nicer moments.

As I watched Aybel and Phoenix saunter off to go and dance with the other fae, I shrugged my shoulders, realising that I had two options. I could stay at the buffet table – watching everyone dance from a distance, I would continue to feel like an outsider, bewildered and uncomfortable in the unfamiliar environment. Alternatively, I could simply embrace the newness of everything around me, accepting that I was no longer under the difficult constraints of life in Blackfern.

I had no idea where I truly wanted to be. Further

to that, it felt unfair that I was in Ovon whilst Lyda – and even Tyal – were still back in Blackfern. I felt guilty to be in such a nice place.

I shook my head determinedly, keen to distract myself from my reverie. Whether I had asked for it or not, here I was. The least I could do was be courteous to my hosts. Having managed to be accepting of Tyal and his awful attitude back in Blackfern, I could easily give Aybel and Phoenix a chance, both of whom had so far, made a real effort to be accommodating and welcoming. In all fairness, they had been nothing but kind to me.

A young fae woman – her wings an iridescent blue and her long flowing hair a bright, bold pink – sang heartily into an amplification device fashioned from hollowed-out bark. Standing on the platform of a large log, as she performed enthusiastically, her passionate vocals rang out across the gathering. The lyrics were proud and inspired:

Oh, great forest of golden sparkle
How we appreciate thee
The joys of life in this here court
And what it is to be free

A loud and appreciative cheer erupted from the crowd. They seemed to like the last line best of all.

I had never heard a song like it before. It didn't sound even close to what would meet approval under the dictatorship in Blackfern.

I nudged my way through the crowd and put my mouth close to Aybel's ear.

"I have to ask," I said quietly. "Is everyone here an activist?"

Aybel didn't seem perturbed by my question. Instead, she acknowledged it with a confident nod of her head, stepping back from me to show that nothing needed to be reduced to a quiet, secretive conversation.

"Some of the fae here are activists. Some of them aren't," she explained. "Whilst some are passionately doing their bit, others just want to live their lives in peace and keep a relatively low profile. Not that I can blame them for that."

"I hope you don't mind me asking," I said. "It's just that… The song that fae was singing: the words seem a bit loaded."

"Hmm…" Aybel mused. "I suppose they could be interpreted that way. The music here is whatever you want it to be though. Perhaps you're just being cynical based on what you're used to in Blackfern."

I felt a little patronised by Aybel's comment. To me, my question had been a reasonable one. As far as I saw it, I was curious about the inspiration behind the music. Well, perhaps my enquiry was *somewhat* deeper than that, but all the same, I hadn't expected Aybel to think of me as being overly cynical.

I chewed on my lower lip, still cautious that I didn't want to seem ungrateful to Aybel and her hospitality. After all, I was in unfamiliar territory; it wouldn't do me any good to come across as confrontational.

Aybel means well, and so does Phoenix. I guess I'm just so damned used to overthinking everything.

I decided to throw caution to the wind. It was time to start enjoying myself. It no longer made sense to try analysing the things beyond my understanding, and beyond my control. It was in that moment that I made a promise to myself.

No matter how, I would one day find some kind of happiness. I had no idea what that would look like. But I needed to *believe* that it would happen. Of course, worries for those who I had left behind in Blackfern were still prominently on my mind. I was still deeply concerned for Lyda in particular.

I just need to be in the moment. That's all I can do right now.

I closed my eyes and spread my arms, swaying with the rhythm of the music and letting it take me away.

In moving with the soothing melodies, I must have veered closer towards the large log upon which the pink-haired fae was still performing. When I opened my eyes to look up at her, I noticed the elaborate patterns on her wings. As she continued to dance, a powerful, mesmerising glow emanated from them. It reminded me of how the fae in Ovon didn't have to hide their magic, or the natural glow of their wings. I had forgotten how majestic it could look; the wings of the fae back in Blackfern had lost their glow long ago.

"Hey," said the fae, reaching down and

charismatically stretching her hand out to greet me. "Come up here and dance with me. Come on, you know you want to."

Her inviting smile was such that I couldn't refuse her offer. I climbed up onto the log, and then turned around to look out at the exuberant crowd. It was a magnificent sight to behold.

I had barely become used to my newfound position when she thrust her amplification device into my hand, giving me no choice but to grab hold of it.

"Sing," she implored. "Sing!"

I had never sung to a large crowd before. Singing quietly in the privacy of my own company had always been a pleasure though.

I stood there for a moment, willing myself to channel some sort of energy. As the band continued playing, so many thoughts flashed through my mind, until all of a sudden, a wave of inspiration crashed over me.

This is my chance to get some clarity.

I took a deep breath and then shouted into the

hollowed-out bark.

"Hey, everyone! Stop the music for a moment. Stop!"

The band gradually petered out. Having acknowledged my words, the crowd looked around quizzically, unsure of what was going on.

"Listen to me. *Please* listen to me, everyone," I said. "I need to talk to you. I've been brought here from Blackfern."

I looked down at Aybel and Phoenix, relieved to observe that they didn't look offended by my announcement. I didn't want to embarrass them, but equally, I knew that if I was going to be in Ovon for a while, I needed to be able to speak – and live – my truth.

I put my mouth back to the bark.

"I've been bought here from Blackfern. How many of you are aware of what's happening there?"

"We're very aware of what's happening in Blackfern," a young fae woman with two young children shouted up at me. "Please don't think that we're not."

"Oh," I said, surprised. "You all look so happy. I hadn't expected everyone here to be so carefree."

"It's not that we choose to ignore the troubles that are going on over the border," the woman replied, keen to defend her stance. "It's just that for our own peace of mind, we can't grieve every day over something that we can't control. We help where we can, and we welcome anyone here who has managed to cross the border. We hope so much that more fae can come here from Blackfern – or better yet, that Blackfern ceases to be the horrible place that it currently is. When all's said and done though, we're just regular fae – with lives that we need to nurture here. We're very aware of the limitations of our own power."

"But I don't understand," I said. "You're all allowed to use magic here. Why don't the fae of Ovon collectively rise in defiance against the dictatorship of Blackfern?"

"Because that would start a war!" she shouted, frustrated. "Why on Earth would you advocate for a war?"

It was a good point, and one that I hadn't thought of before. The fae of Ovon were not at fault for embracing the opportunity to enjoy their lives. Just like the fae of Blackfern, they had not been given a choice in their place of birth.

"For my entire life, under the regime of Blackfern, I've had to suppress my magic," I said. "Seeing all of you here today reminds me of what it means to be a fae. Not only that, but what it means to be a *free* fae. None of you have been bullied into denying your magic. You've all been able to *nurture* it, and it hasn't died. Together, you're so powerful that you could probably topple the dictatorship of Blackfern if you put your minds to it!"

"But we don't want a war!" a burly male fae in the crowd shouted out, clearly annoyed by my suggestion.

His point was a valid one. It was only natural for fae in a peaceful court to be against the idea of risking a war with Blackfern.

"I understand what you're saying," I said. "Really, I do. I know that everybody wants to live in peace. I just find it so hard to observe that here you all are with so much, and in contrast to that, the fae of Blackfern have so little."

"Are you trying to make us feel guilty?" another male fae shouted out from the back of the crowd.

"No, no. Not at all," I implored. "Please, you must understand that less than a couple of days ago, I was brought over the border from Blackfern into Ovon. I've never been anywhere else in my life. I was born in Blackfern, and I thought that's where I would stay forever. I've never seen anything like this before. Please, I'm just so overwhelmed; I'm just trying to make sense of it all."

"We hear you," said the woman as she held her two children closely to her. "Really, we do. We want to support you. We want to help you. We're not upset with what you're saying. How you feel is entirely understandable. You've lived your whole life under a cruel dictatorship, and here you are experiencing a complete culture shock."

Exhausted, I put a hand up to my head and gripped my hair in frustration.

"I just want the fae I've left behind in Blackfern

to be safe, and *free*," I said. "*Please*, won't you help them?"

I hadn't wanted to beg, but I couldn't bear the thought of Lyda having to stay behind in Blackfern – not when just within walking distance, the fae of Ovon were free.

"We're not denying what the fae of Blackfern are up against," another male fae spoke up. "It's just that we're simply not prepared to be pressured into having a war that frankly, we're not sure we could win."

I didn't know what to say to that. All I could do was grunt in exasperation. I was certain that by this point, I had probably alienated an entire community.

"If you want to rally against the kingdom of Blackfern, go and do it yourself," said a particularly skinny, older male fae. "We understand that you're angry, but we simply cannot afford to risk our lives in a quest that could prove to be futile."

"But you've got all your magic and you can use that," I said. "Maybe none of you truly understand just how dire the situation in

Blackfern is."

"We understand," said the man, his tone blunt and dismissive. "Don't insult our intelligence."

"Ok," I replied, taking a deep breath and trying to stay calm. "You *might* understand it, I'll give you that, but you haven't lived it. I'm begging you all, *please*, even if you can't help the whole of Blackfern, could you at least help me to get my cousin over the border?"

Nobody responded to my plea. I could feel a torrent of anger stirring inside me.

"I appreciate that none of you are to blame for what's happening in Blackfern," I reasoned. "I don't want you to feel guilty for the fact that you have a nice life here in Ovon. I know that some of you are working hard and taking incredible risks to help a few individuals here and there. I just wish that more could be done to help *everyone* in Blackfern."

From within the restless crowd, I could see Phoenix and Aybel coming up towards me. Taking a side each, they both put an arm around me, and then assertively guided me off and away from my platform.

"Come on, Skyler," Phoenix said, leaning in closely towards me. "Take some deep breaths. You need to calm down and be sensible about this."

Although he was trying to be helpful, his words triggered me like nothing else had since I'd first arrived in Ovon.

"No!" I shouted, abruptly brushing him – and Aybel – away. "I can't possibly think about staying here in Ovon and building a life here for myself when I know full well that the fae I grew up with in Blackfern are stuck there and having an awful time of it. How can I live happily – and without fear – when my mind is plagued by the guilt of that?! I won't be able to live with myself until I've at least *tried* to do something to help the fae of Blackfern. I know you're both trying your best, and it was never my intention to suggest otherwise. For me though, I can't settle whilst knowing that there's more to be done!"

"Fine," said the elderly man from the crowd who had already made his position clear. "If you want a war, go and have one on your own."

Chapter Eight

I ran back to the cottage at such speed that I had no idea if Aybel and Phoenix were following behind me. I didn't care either. When I got to the front door, I pushed it open with such force that it slammed against the wall and shook on its hinges.

I sat down on a kitchen chair, and, placing my elbows on the table, I buried my head in my hands. Deep, angry sobs coursed through my entire being. I couldn't shake the feeling that something was very wrong; not only was I in an unfamiliar place, but I had alienated the entire community.

I'll never be able to build a life here now.

Knowing what I had left behind in Blackfern, and of how I had no chance of being happy in Ovon, I pounded my fist down against the wooden table, causing it to vibrate.

Sighing and putting the fallen candlesticks back in their holders, as I looked around the room, I reminded myself that Aybel and Phoenix's hospitality might not be limitless. I still needed to respect their home, even if they were about to throw me out based on what I'd said to the crowd of fae in the forest.

I got up and began to pace around the room, keen to expel even just some of the pent-up emotion charging through me. I could soon hear voices coming from outside. Phoenix and Aybel then entered the cottage, and with them, was a large group of fae. I recognised them all from the gathering in the forest.

Oh no! This is it! Something awful is about to happen! They look so fired-up right now – and it's all my fault!

"Please don't hurt me," I begged feebly. "I'm so sorry. I didn't mean to upset any of you. I didn't mean to disrespect your hospitality, or the efforts that must have been taken to get me over the border. Please know that I really do appreciate it, and that I'm so sorry."

I found myself desperately backing away into a corner at the other end of the kitchen. As I looked at the faces of everyone observing me, they seemed confused.

"Nobody wants to hurt you. Nobody wants to do anything bad to you," Phoenix said, his tone calm, yet assertive. "Sit down and calm down. We're going to talk about this properly."

"Ok," I replied, still on edge.

Normally, I would have felt patronised and annoyed at Phoenix's tone and domineering manner. In being so worked-up though, it was a relief to be told that nobody wanted to do anything horrible to me.

I sat down at the table again.

"Skyler, we're not upset with you," Aybel soothed as she smiled at me reassuringly. "We just want to talk to you."

"Ok," I said. "First though, I want to apologise to all of you. I didn't mean to disrespect any of your values, or the way that any of you choose to live your lives. After all, the circumstances in which you live are a result of where you were born – and that's something that nobody can control. It's not my place to resent you for the fact that you have always lived somewhere nicer than I have. I'm sorry I asked you all to fight on my behalf. You've got your own lives and your own loved ones. I shouldn't expect you to sacrifice yourselves just because I'm angry about what's happening back in Blackfern."

Keen to assert himself, a middle-aged male fae stepped confidently forward from the group.

"Actually, we've been thinking," he said. "We simply can't ignore what you've told us. Whilst we can't allow ourselves to feel guilty for having a nice life here in Ovon, the fact is that we could do more to help the fae of Blackfern. We don't want to go to war. *Nobody* in their right mind wants to go to war. All the same though, we appreciate what you've said and we'd like to discuss it further."

Surprised by his stance and trying to take it all in, I tentatively chewed on my lower lip. Considering that I'd interrupted their joyous gathering in order to lecture them, I hadn't expected the fae of Ovon to be willing to take me seriously.

"The fae of Ovon are lucky," he continued. "We have always been able to use our magic; it has been all too easy for us to forget what it must be like for the fae of Blackfern. It must feel awful to have the potential for magic coursing through your veins, and then having to suppress it by order of the dictatorship. We have been thinking about what you said – in that perhaps if we all got together and used our magic at the same time, we could help to make a difference."

I was hanging on his every word.

"Even if we can't use our magic to topple Blackfern's dictatorship entirely, there is still hope that we could use it to help more fae cross over the border into Ovon," he added. "By getting as many fae as possible out of Blackfern, then perhaps one day, the population under the dictatorship would be too small to wage a war against us here. Not only that, but upon helping the Blackfern fae into Ovon, we would like to build more homes and expand our own community. For us, it's not about acquiring more potential soldiers. We simply want to save as many fae as we possibly can, and we've got the space here in the court of Ovon to facilitate that."

"That's amazing!" I enthused. "If fae from both Blackfern and Ovon can gather at the border, the Ovon fae could all use their magic at the same time to create a barrier through which everybody could cross safely from Blackfern. Of course, there's no way of knowing how the guards in Blackfern will react. Some would probably be insistent on following the regime's orders. That said, I'm sure there are those who would jump at the opportunity to escape – even after having been compliant and seemingly loyal to the king. If everyone capable of it uses their magic at the same time, I'm sure there is hope of being able to free those who wish to leave Blackfern."

Everyone nodded in agreement.

"Hang on a minute though," I said. "How on Earth would we be able to get a message over to the fae of Blackfern: one informing them that they need to rally around and gather at the border at a particular time? It's the sort of message that could easily cause trouble, especially in the hands of those who might wish to sabotage it. There's a lot that could go wrong here."

"I think you just need to believe in the goodwill

of the majority," Phoenix said firmly. "You're right to consider that nobody can predict or control how the fae of Blackfern might respond to a message from Ovon, especially considering the nature of it. Some fae might be too set in their ways, preferring to remain in Blackfern. I am certain though, that many would be elated at being offered the chance of freedom. We're in control of the fact that we can give them an opportunity. What they do with it is up to them."

"How exactly are we going to get a message into Blackfern?" I asked, not wanting to lose sight of the danger of what could happen if it all went wrong.

Aybel sighed heavily. She then put her hand on my shoulder, and spoke reluctantly.

"That's where you come in, Skyler. You're right to question how we could ever get such a message to so many fae in Blackfern. It would need to be heard by many – and in such a short space of time too! Realistically, our only hope is your connection to Lyda."

"Lyda?!" I exclaimed, alarmed that the stakes were becoming so rapidly high, and personal. "Why Lyda?!"

"Well," said Phoenix. "You know how you mentioned to us that you had told her you were going to the border?"

"Yes," I answered suspiciously, suddenly anxious about what they were about to ask of me.

"If Lyda is your most reliable ally in Blackfern, then surely she will be the best point of contact."

I could feel my enthusiasm for the whole thing beginning to wane.

"Hang on," I demanded. "You're basically saying to me that I should use my magic to send a telepathic message to Lyda in the hope that she – and she alone – can rally everyone from Blackfern to the border."

"That's about the size of it," Phoenix said frankly.

A bolt of panic shot through me. The plan no longer felt simple. The risk was tremendous. If something went wrong and the king was to find out about Lyda's role in the whole thing, she would be in grave danger. I had absolutely no doubt about that. The dictatorship would regard imprisonment as an insufficient punishment; she would certainly be put to death.

"Ok," I said with a sigh, frightened and doubtful. "I need you all to realise the magnitude of what you're asking me to do here. You're asking me to put Lyda's life on the line. She's my cousin, and I care about her. She has always been on my side. I don't know if it's right for me to volunteer her into such a dangerous position."

A younger male fae spoke up, a slight tone of anger in his voice.

"You need to realise that this isn't easy for us either," he said. "If the plan were to go incredibly wrong, the fae of Ovon could find themselves at war with Blackfern – and one hell of a war it would be! There is an element of risk involved for everybody, and although that risk looks different for each of us, it is nevertheless still there. We all need to put our faith into this, and give it our all, if it is to work. Of course, thinking about this positively, if we *do* manage to get the majority of fae from Blackfern over the border, then the scope for war would no longer be there; it would simply be impossible for the king – he would no longer have enough soldiers to fight for the dictatorship."

"I hear what you're saying," I said. "Really, I do. *Please* though, can I just have a night to think about this? Deep down, to the very core of my being, I know that the right thing to do is to liberate as many fae from Blackfern as we possibly can. I *know* that. But please, I'm begging you. I just need one night to think this all over. I need to ask myself: if this were to go wrong, and if Lyda's life were to be sacrificed to something that she had never asked for, could I live with myself?"

Phoenix addressed the gathered fae.

"Skyler is right," he said. "Whether or not this whole thing can go ahead rests entirely on her decision. We shouldn't underestimate the pressure on her. Whatever choice she makes, it needs to feel right for her. I know there are more of you, and it's great that you're all on board, but we can't force Skyler into putting her cousin in danger. None of us have walked in her shoes."

"I agree," said Aybel, taking me by the hand and giving it a reassuring squeeze. "This isn't about making anybody feel obliged to do anything. If we're all going to group together to do this, we *all* need to be able to move with conviction, rather than with regret."

"Ok," said the younger male fae, solemn, yet proudly having appointed himself as spokesperson for the group of fae behind him. "I can't deny you any of that. I agree with your stance. We will bid you good day. Tomorrow, we will return for an answer."

84

Chapter Nine

The following morning, I woke with a start.

This is happening! This is really happening!

My sleep had been turbulent at best, but it wasn't due to me being uncertain of what I should do. More than anything, I had been fired-up since the fae of Ovon had left me to think about the plan.

Respectful of the space I had asked for, Aybel and Phoenix had camped out in the forest overnight. Although I had been home alone for a while, it hadn't taken me long to come to a decision.

As frightened as I was about the risk of implicating Lyda if the plan were to go drastically wrong, I knew deep in my heart that I had to embrace the opportunity to liberate as many fae as possible. I knew I would feel awful if things went wrong, but I also knew that I wouldn't be able to live with myself if I didn't at least try. In Blackfern, there were many lives at stake under such an evil dictatorship. With that in mind, I had made a promise to myself to do what would be best for the greater good.

As I enjoyed the comforting warmth of the abundant duvet on top of me, I noticed that the sun was still rising. Unable to get back to sleep though, I got up, and then set about making myself a generous, healthy breakfast of crumpets and blueberry tea. I knew that I would need much stamina, not only for being able to channel my magic, but in order to think straight and rationally.

It had been such a long time since I'd used my magic to telepathically communicate with anybody. Such a thing had been banned in Blackfern long ago. As young children, although it was natural for all fae to explore the abilities they had been born with, upon starting school under the dictatorship, everyone was taught to never use them again. As a result, although each and every fae in Blackfern had an awareness of their innate propensity to perform magic, whether or not they would be confident with it years later, after having had it trained out of them, was a different matter entirely.

I knew that not only would I have to search deep within myself to access that kind of magic, but I would also have to take a chance on the hope that Lyda would be able to *receive* a telepathic message, having compliantly suppressed her own magic for so many years.

Taking a deep breath to control my whirling thoughts, I reminded myself that the strong rapport I shared with Lyda would be advantageous. We had often had moments where she had been able to sense what I was thinking. Overall, I had to trust that although she hadn't consented to what was about to happen, she would be capable of engaging with it.

Throughout the night, I had played many hypothetical conversations in my mind of what Lyda might say to me in the event of us being reunited in Ovon. In some of the conversations, she was angry, her tone laced with a feeling of betrayal, but in others, she was happy and relieved. For my own sanity, I then had to focus only on what could go right, rather than on what could go horribly, horribly wrong.

With no one around to see just how rusty I had become, I figured that it was the perfect opportunity to at least practice my magic.

I'll try getting a message out to Aybel and Phoenix, telling them to come home because I've made breakfast. There's plenty left, and I'm sure they'll appreciate it.

I closed my eyes and beat my wings together, an overwhelming tension running through my body. I could feel a warmth coursing through every fibre of my being, giving me hope that from somewhere deep within, I could channel what had been suppressed for so long.

Surrounded by the beginnings of a bright light, I squeezed every muscle tightly, balling my fists aggressively until the heat running through my arms felt almost intolerable. Nevertheless, despite my unfamiliarity with the intense sensation, I put every ounce of passion into accessing that vital essence of my fae identity.

As the glow surrounding me became more vibrant, I worked hard to get the message to Aybel. I thought the words that I needed her to hear, hoping that she would latch on to them from her side of the forest. Although the message was simple and not particularly essential in and of itself, it was imperative for me to test whether my magic still worked.

Having done all that I could, I opened my eyes. I quickly closed them again as the room started to spin, a wave of nausea hitting me like a tidal wave. Drained by the strength of the magic that I had become so unused to drawing out, my entire body suddenly felt stone cold. Exhausted, I dropped to my knees and put my head in my hands.

Just from the sensations I was experiencing, I knew that my magic was *somewhere* out there, echoing through the airwaves of the forest. However, I had no idea of whether I had been successful in my direction of the message; was it now with Aybel, or had I lost the ability to be fully in command of my magic?

Chapter Ten

There were so many unknowns. With my mind having wandered off into a blend of daydreams, I had lost track of the time. Eventually, I was distracted from my reverie when the front door burst open, and in charged Aybel and Phoenix.

"You did it, Skyler! You did it!" Aybel enthused loudly. "I knew you could. We're so proud of you."

"What?" I said, bewildered and a little overwhelmed.

"I got your message," said Aybel.

"My magic still works!" I exclaimed, not quite daring to believe it.

"Yes," Aybel answered, fluttering her wings excitedly.

"That's such a relief," I said. "I knew you would both be coming back to the cottage anyway, but I figured that if I could just send you a simple message…"

"About the breakfast?" Aybel interrupted.

"Yes, that's the one," I replied. "I figured that if I could send you that, then I would be able to prove to myself that my magic still works. This is exactly the reassurance I need. When it comes to sending a message to Lyda, the stakes are so much higher and I need to get it right."

"You've done the right thing," said Phoenix. "Now you know that you can do it, you can rule out some of your fears about communicating with Lyda. The last thing any of us wants would be for somebody with ill intentions to intercept it."

"The understanding that Lyda and I share has always been strong, and although she hasn't used her magic since it was trained out of her as a child, I'm certain that she will receive the message I send," I said. "The more I think about what we're about to do, the more I believe in it."

"I knew you'd come around," said Aybel.

"I mean, don't misunderstand," I said. "I'm still scared. In fact, in view of what we're hoping to achieve, I think it would be concerning if we didn't feel at least a little bit of fear. What matters though, is that I *can* use my magic, and I *can* get that message through to Lyda."

"This is brilliant," said Phoenix. "There's every hope that we'll be able to liberate enough fae from Blackfern that even when it angers the king, there won't be enough of a population remaining to fight a war against Ovon."

"You know," I said. "I feel proud that I'm still able to use my magic. I've managed to reignite the spark that I was born with, and indeed, a vital part of my fae identity. It means a lot to me. For Blackfern to train it out of us as children, it isn't natural, it isn't right. Nobody asked for it to be that way, and yet for generations it has been taken as the accepted way of doing things. I want more fae to be free – free from fear, and free to embrace the power of their magic."

"Now then," said Phoenix, his tone suddenly more serious. "Is there anything more we can do to give you the best chance of being able to get the message over to Lyda?"

"Well," I said. "I hope neither of you mind, but I was able to use my magic with nobody else around. Would you both be ok that I request to be left alone when I send the message to Lyda. It might sound a bit silly, but I don't want to feel self-conscious or distracted. With no room for error, I need to focus on giving it my all."

"I agree," said Aybel. "We all need to do whatever it takes to give this the best chance of working."

"Another thing," I said. "We need to make sure that we give Lyda enough time to get the fae of Blackfern to group together. In view of how she is still under the dictatorship, what we're asking her to do is tremendous. Still though, I know she'll need to move quickly."

With expressions of understanding etched on their faces, both Aybel and Phoenix nodded in agreement.

"Realistically, I think we should ask Lyda to gather the fae of Blackfern at the border in five days' time," I said. "I know that doesn't sound too generous, but with each day that passes, the risk of the information falling into the wrong hands will increase. For us, the wait will be horrible. We'll have no way of being able to tell what's happening over there. If it is going wrong, we probably won't find out about it until it's too late – perhaps not even until, God forbid, a war is waged against Ovon."

"That's a good point," said Phoenix. "There are many things to consider here."

"There are," Aybel said solemnly.

"I know," I said. "Thanks to both of you though, I believe in what we're doing. At that gathering in the forest, when I witnessed the freedom the fae of Ovon have, it made me yearn so deeply to see that same freedom bestowed upon the fae of Blackfern. I want this to work, and surely that alone gives us an advantage. We *believe* in the importance of freedom."

96

Chapter Eleven

Ever since I had sent the message to Lyda, the wait had been agonising. The fear of the unknown had cast a dark shadow over all of us. Tensions were high in the cottage – so much so that, beyond preparing for our trip to the border, nobody had spoken much to each other.

When the crucial day finally arrived, all we could do was hope that the fae of Blackfern would be there to meet us at the border. We had done all we could to prepare. Energised to use all of our magic combined, we were ready to create a safe barrier through which the fae wishing to escape Blackfern could cross. Simply by the sheer number of Ovon fae who had promised to engage, the guards of Blackfern wouldn't stand a chance. We even held on to the hope that the guards themselves would take the opportunity to cross over into Ovon.

Of course, we were highly aware that upon getting to the border, the fae of Ovon could be disappointed to observe that nobody from Blackfern had come to meet us. In such case, we would have to assume the worst: that Lyda had been caught and punished not long after having received the message, or that during her efforts to gather the fae of Blackfern, something had gone wrong along the way.

When I had sent the message to Lyda, I had made it clear to her that she wasn't to get back in touch with me. For her to use her magic, if indeed she still could, was far too dangerous. I couldn't bear the thought of her getting caught in the act.

And so, as Phoenix, Aybel and I packed our bags and prepared to leave the cottage in order to meet the other fae of Ovon at the border, all we could do was hope. The rest of it was out of our hands.

As we walked through the forest towards the border, we all looked at each other solemnly, prepared for what we needed to do, and yet anxious of what could be up ahead. We had no idea what to expect. Trying to steady my nerves, I looked around at the trees and foliage surrounding us. Splinters of sunlight sparkled through from gaps between the branches that hung above, and along with the sweet melodies of birdsong, the forest seemed so humble, so peaceful. It felt strange to consider the calming bliss in comparison to the extremity of what we were planning to do.

From the pathways of dry mud leading into other parts of Ovon, I could see more fae emerging. Knowing that they had determinedly left their own homes in preparation to face the unknown so bravely, I felt a strong sense of camaraderie.

Not only are the fae of Ovon on my side, they're on the side of the greater good overall. We're all in this together, doing it to save our fellow fae in the hope that it will set up future generations for a better way of life.

As she walked alongside me, Aybel gave my hand a reassuring squeeze. It had become something of a habit for her, and one that I had grown to welcome. Her presence could be so comforting.

"We're going to do our very best," she said. "No matter what happens today, none of us can look back and say that we didn't try."

She was right. I promised myself that I would hold on to her words, regardless of what was in store.

The group of fae marching stoically alongside us had grown larger in number. There were many men and women from at least three different generations, all ready to support the cause. It was humbling and only served to add to the nervous lump in my throat, my mouth feeling as dry as ash as the border and the outer limits of Blackfern came into view.

"Listen!" commanded Phoenix, his voice low. "Can you hear that?"

As we all stood still and fell urgently silent, we could hear footsteps. The sound was coming from Blackfern.

"You all know what this means," Aybel said quietly. "The fae of Blackfern must be coming to meet us at the border. Assuming that it's not a gathering of enemy soldiers, this is it; this is our chance to help good fae cross over into Ovon."

"Ok," Phoenix whispered determinedly. "When I say so, all of you need to channel your magic over into Blackfern. Just like we've planned, we're all going to summon our powers at the same time. Then, with the force of the glow that emerges, we'll create a barrier through which the fae of Blackfern can cross safely over the border to us. Be ready to do this at any moment."

The steely tension in the air was like nothing I had ever felt before.

Shocked to witness the large crowd of fae that were moving in droves towards the edge of the Blackfern border, I remained poised, ready to draw on my magic at short notice. Although I had tensed my muscles and was bracing myself, I couldn't help but tilt my head up, keen to examine the continuously emerging crowd. In my desperation to see Lyda, I found myself silently praying to an unknown god.

Please let Lyda be amongst those fae. Please let them all cross safely into Ovon.

Not wishing to lose hope, and needing to stay focused in order to engage my magic, I reminded myself that at minimum, Lyda must have received my message and had been successful in gathering the heaving crowd of fae that was coming towards us.

Upon hearing Phoenix's loud command, I was immediately distracted from my thoughts.

"Now everybody! Now! Use your magic *now*!"

Straight away, with absolute passion, I closed my eyes tightly and beat my wings furiously. As much as I was shocked by the warmth coming from my own body, it was nothing compared to the heat of the collective glow coming from all of the fae around me.

I continued to move my wings with fervour. As I held on to the urgent feeling of what needed to be done, my life – along with a vast array of the horrors that the fae of Blackfern had suffered – flashed before my eyes.

I wasn't just doing this for Lyda; I was doing this in honour of my parents, and for the generations of fae before them who had also had to suffer under the dictatorship. I was even doing this for Tyal; no fae, whether I truly liked them or not, deserved to live under such brutal conditions.

Just like the fae around me, I beat my wings even harder. The intensity of the heat around us continued to increase. I didn't dare to look, but I was certain that the magic we were generating would soon be forming a force field through which the Blackfern fae could cross.

Suddenly, I heard an ear-shattering scream. I sharply looked around to see who could be in trouble, my focus no longer on my magic.

It was Aybel! It took me a while to register the sight before me. She was stumbling away from the crowd and towards the ground, cradling one arm in the other. She had clearly taken a hit.

"Are you ok?" I asked frantically, crouching down to check on her.

"My arm…" she said, breathing heavily as she nodded towards the long arrow that had penetrated the flesh of her forearm.

Realising that the arrow had come from Blackfern, a tornado of white-hot rage tore through me.

"What the hell is wrong with you?" I bellowed out in the direction of Blackfern. "We're trying to *help* you!"

"Who the hell do you think you are?" a shrill voice shouted hysterically from across the border. "What makes you think that everyone in Blackfern wants to leave?! Why don't you morons go back to Ovon and leave us alone."

"Don't be ridiculous," I retorted. "You don't have to agree with what we're doing, but why try and harm us in the process?"

Aybel had been so good to me. I couldn't bear to think that she was in pain. Instinctively, I turned to give her my full attention.

"I'm going to help you," I said determinedly as I looked with confidence into her panic-stricken eyes. "It looks like the arrow hasn't gone in too deeply. I think if I'm especially careful, I could probably remove it without causing further damage."

"I don't know," said Aybel. "It really hurts."

"Bastards!" I exclaimed, livid that a Blackfern fae had the gall to stoop so low.

"It's ok," said Aybel, her tone calm and

considered despite the situation. "I'm angry too, but I can understand it. We've got to remember that the fae of Blackfern have lived under the thumb of the dictatorship for so long that they might truly believe they're better off there; they genuinely might see us as a threat."

Impressed by Aybel's ability to reason whilst she was in pain, I chewed anxiously on my lower lip.

"In normal circumstances, I would much rather wait for a medic to remove this arrow," she said, turning her full attention to her wound. "These aren't normal circumstances though, so I guess we have no choice."

"I promise I'll do my best for you," I said. "Close your eyes and remember that once it's out, the worst of the pain will be over."

Chapter Twelve

As much as it had pained her, I had managed to get the arrow out of Aybel's arm. Just as we had been hoping for, the wound wasn't too deep. From the trunk of one of the trees nearby, I'd grabbed a strip of rainbow eucalyptus bark to rub onto the injury and surrounding area. With the strong essence of magic all around us, she would heal soon enough.

"We'd better get back to the group," I said. "We've completely lost track of what's happening."

"Right," Aybel replied. "Phoenix will be in control. Our absence hasn't been ideal, but with so many fae using their magic together, I sense that at minimum, the force field will remain for a while yet."

Together, with our heads held high, we marched determinedly back towards the fae of Ovon, who were still bathed in the warming light of magic.

When we rejoined the crowd, we noticed that it was larger than before.

This can only mean one thing. Many fae must have crossed over from Blackfern.

"I'd like to know the whereabouts of that idiot who shot the arrow," I wondered aloud, not expecting an answer.

"I wouldn't worry about it," said Aybel. "Whoever they are, I feel sorry for them – not so much in terms of how they've made themselves unpopular, but because upon being given an opportunity for a better way of life, instead of giving it a chance, they have responded with violence. Not everyone wants change. It's their loss more than mine."

Suddenly, from within the bustling crowd, Phoenix came running towards us.

"We've done it! We've done it!" he exclaimed in elation. "The Blackfern fae have crossed over the border. From what I've heard so far, I don't think the entire population wanted to come. It seems to be the majority who have though. Take a look around – so many are now free from the dictatorship. And hey, Skyler, I've got someone who wants to say hello to you."

He charged back into the bustling crowd. I hoped so badly that he was about to bring Lyda to meet me.

And then, sure enough, he came running back towards me, guiding Lyda by the hand behind him. I ran to her immediately. So much had happened since we had last seen each other that neither of us had the words to articulate how we were feeling. We simply held each other in a tight embrace.

Still in shock that we were together again, we finally let go. As we took a step back from each other and made eye contact, we revelled in the joyful realisation that we were not only reunited, but safe.

"It's over!" said Lyda, ecstatic and relieved. "It's really over! We did it! We don't have to be afraid anymore."

"You must have gone through so much to make this happen," I said. "I still can't believe you're here."

"It wasn't easy," she replied. "Fortunately though, the vast majority of Blackfern wanted to escape. Those who objected were in such a minority that there was everything to play for. So many fae wanted to grab the chance to move to Ovon that they made it their mission to silence those who were against what we were plotting. Collectively, we all put our heads together, and with the help of the magic from Ovon's fae – and yours, of course – we were able to cross the border. There weren't enough guards to stop us."

"Did any of the guards come over with you?" I asked.

"They did," said Lyda. "Oh, and speaking of the king's now former employees, I think Tyal is amongst them."

"Oh," I said.

"Hey, aren't you happy that he's free?" she asked.

"Of course I am," I said. "It's just that I don't wish to see him right now – or perhaps, ever again."

"You don't need to worry about him anymore," said Lyda. "You are no longer under obligation to be with him. Now that we're all in Ovon, the rules of Blackfern's dictatorship don't apply."

"We will do everything we can to help everyone settle in," said Phoenix. "It will be a pleasure, and an honour."

"Is there anyone left behind in Blackfern who doesn't want to be there?" I asked.

"Everyone who wanted to cross into Ovon has done so," Lyda explained. "Those who insisted on staying in Blackfern are in such a minority that even if the king ordered them to fight, there's nothing that could be done to his advantage. He wouldn't stand a chance. Besides, many of us are looking forward to using our magic again now that we're in Ovon. This newfound freedom means we can begin to live in a way that is true to ourselves. Never again will we have to suppress the magic that has been in our blood for generations."

"Perhaps one day, the fae of Ovon – that's all of us now – will be able to reclaim the land in Blackfern," said Phoenix. "However, what matters for now, is that the regime is no longer a threat. The King of Blackfern can live out his life there, stewing in the very misery that so many fae are now liberated from."

Feeling overjoyed by what we had achieved, and basking in the sheer triumph and excitement of the moment, Phoenix, Aybel, Lyda and I grabbed on to each other in a friendly, emotionally-fuelled embrace. The future was looking bright.

Chapter Twelve

www.ingramcontent.com/pod-product-compliance
Lightning Source LLC
Chambersburg PA
CBHW050441200726
48295CB00024B/883